Time Jumpers

STEALING THE SWORD

by
WENDY MASS

illustrated by
ORIOL VIDAL

BRANCHES
SCHOLASTIC INC.

Read all the

Time Jumpers

adventures!

More books coming soon!

scholastic.com/timejumpers

Table of Contents

For Katie and Rachel, thank you for
jumping through time with me! **—WM**

To my family, the best ones **—OV**

Text copyright © 2018 by Wendy Mass
Illustrations by Oriol Vidal copyright © 2018 by Scholastic Inc.

All rights reserved. Published by Scholastic Inc., *Publishers since 1920.* SCHOLASTIC, BRANCHES, and associated logos are trademarks and/or registered trademarks of Scholastic Inc.

The publisher does not have any control over and does not assume any responsibility for author or third-party websites or their content.

No part of this publication may be reproduced, stored in a retrieval system, or transmitted in any form or by any means, electronic, mechanical, photocopying, recording, or otherwise, without written permission of the publisher. For information regarding permission, write to Scholastic Inc., Attention: Permissions Department, 557 Broadway, New York, NY 10012.

This book is a work of fiction. Names, characters, places, and incidents are either the product of the author's imagination or are used fictitiously, and any resemblance to actual persons, living or dead, business establishments, events, or locales is entirely coincidental.

Library of Congress Cataloging-in-Publication Data

Names: Mass, Wendy, 1967- author. | Vidal, Oriol, 1977- illustrator.
Title: Stealing the sword! / by Wendy Mass ; illustrated by Oriol Vidal.
Description: First edition. | New York, NY : Branches/Scholastic Inc., 2018. | Series: Time Jumpers ; 1 | Summary: At the flea market nine-and-a-half-year-old Chase and his younger sister, Ava, acquire an old suitcase filled with rows of carefully packed strange objects, and when they handle one of the objects (a dragon-headed doorknob) they find themselves in King Arthur's castle, on a mission to save the King—and pursued by a strange man whom they first saw at the flea market, who is after their suitcase.
Identifiers: LCCN 2017041938 | ISBN 9781338217360 (pbk : alk. paper) | ISBN 9781338217377 (hjk : alk. paper)
Subjects: LCSH: Arthur, King—Juvenile fiction. | Merlin (Legendary character)—Juvenile fiction. | Time travel—Juvenile fiction. | Magic—Juvenile fiction. | Swords—Juvenile fiction. | Adventure stories. | CYAC: Arthur, King—Fiction. | Merlin (Legendary character)—Fiction. | Time travel—Fiction. | Magic—Fiction. | Swords—Fiction. | Adventure and adventurers—Fiction. | GSAFD: Adventure fiction. | LCGFT: Action and adventure fiction.
Classification: LCC PZ7.M42355 St 2018 | DDC 813.54 [Fic] —dc23
LC record available at https://lccn.loc.gov/2017041938

10 9 8 7 6 5 4 3 2 1   18 19 20 21 22

Printed in China 62
First edition, September 2018
Edited by Katie Carella
Book design by Sunny Lee

chapter 1

The Adventure Begins!

"Sold!" Chase shouts. His younger sister, Ava, hands the cat sculpture to their latest happy customer. Ever since Chase turned nine and a half his parents have let him and Ava help out at their flea market booth. This made their *fourth* sale today — they'd also sold two chipmunks, an elf, and a tree!

Some people might think you can't make art out of string, playing cards, marbles, candy bar wrappers, and rubber bands. But you totally can.

"Your parents *made* these sculptures?" the woman asks, handing her money to Chase.

"Yup," Chase replies. "Where most people see trash, our parents see treasure. They call it *found art*."

He doesn't mention that when Ava was little, she called it *fart* for short. This made them all laugh, even Mom, who claimed she was only coughing.

"Our parents' regular jobs are pretty stressful," Ava adds, handing the woman her change. "They carry briefcases and wear boring shoes." She wrinkles her nose like she smells something bad. Chase tries not to laugh. No one would ever call his sister's rhinestone-covered tie-dyed sneakers *boring*.

The woman hugs her new purchase as she walks away. Ava snaps a picture with the camera she keeps around her neck.

Click!

Chase high-fives Ava just as their mom turns around.

"You two are getting along nicely," she says.

"We make a good team," Chase admits.

"Mom, the flea market closes soon. Can Chase and I go shop at the other booths?" Ava asks.

Their mom hands them four dollars each. "Stick together and be home by five for dinner."

"We will," Chase promises.

Chase and Ava hop on their bikes and ride deep into the flea market.

Who knows what treasures they'll find?
Or what will find *them*!

chapter 2

An Old Suitcase

Chase stops at a used-books table and spots the perfect book — *101 Funny Facts from History*. He loves facts and he loves history! And who doesn't like to laugh?

"Hey, Ava," Chase says, "which president wore the biggest gloves? Give up? The one with the biggest hands!"

Ava groans and gets in line for funnel cake.

At the next few booths, Chase gets a stack of comic books, a bag of dice, and a Rubik's Cube. He runs out of money after buying a plastic dinosaur with moveable legs.

Ava buys a pair of oversized sunglasses, a picture frame, and a tie-dyed tutu (to match her sneakers).

"I still have one dollar left," she says.

"Your bike basket won't hold all of this stuff," Chase says. His eyes land on a brown suitcase. It's a little bigger than the briefcase his dad carries to work, but much, MUCH cooler.

"We could use that," Ava says, pointing at the exact same suitcase.

They rush over to it.

The suitcase is even more interesting up close. The corners are banged up and the handle is worn. The stickers on the front are torn and faded, but Chase can still make out EGYPT, LONDON, ROME, and SOUTH DAKOTA.

"That one's not supposed to be here," the young woman selling the suitcases says. "The lock is jammed. There is no way to open it."

But Ava says, "Can I try?"

"Sorry, it's just not for sale." The woman turns away to help another customer.

Ava sinks to her knees and touches her fingertips to the lock. She looks up at Chase. "Did you feel that?"

"Feel what?" Chase asks, kneeling beside her.

"Like a chill going through you?" she asks.

"I didn't feel anything," Chase says, not too worried. He's used to Ava's big imagination.

Ava touches the lock again. She presses harder this time. With a soft **WHOOSH** and a louder **CLICK**, the lock springs open!

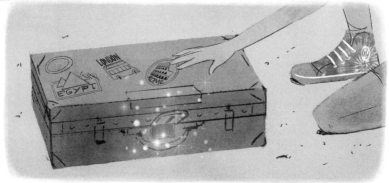

Dinosaurs in Common

"It worked!" Ava shouts. "I unlocked the suitcase!"

The woman working at the booth turns around. "How'd you do that?"

"The lock just opened when I touched it. Now can we buy the suitcase?" Ava starts to lift the lid, but the woman reaches down and snaps it closed.

"Sorry," she says, taking the suitcase by the handle. "The original owner would never want me to sell it."

Chase is disappointed. But he stands up and says, "I understand. Last year, my mom sold my dinosaur puzzle without asking. Even though I don't do jigsaw puzzles much anymore, she knows how much I like dinosaurs."

"He *loves* dinosaurs," Ava corrects as she gets to her feet. "He never goes anywhere without his dinosaur hat."

The woman looks at Chase's hat. "Where did you get that?"

"I got my hat on a class trip to the Natural History Museum," he replies. "One of the scientists there gave it to me."

"Tell her why, Chase," Ava says. "It's kind of a big deal."

Chase reddens.

The woman tilts her head, waiting.

Chase looks down. "I pointed out that they had the bones of the brontosaurus labeled as belonging to the apatosaurus. Someone had made a mistake because the —"

"Brontosaurus got its name back," the woman finishes.

"Exactly!" Chase says, raising his head in surprise.

She smiles. "I like dinosaurs, too. My name is Madeline."

"I'm Chase," he replies, "and this is my younger sister, Ava."

"Only younger by thirteen months," Ava is quick to add as usual.

"I think maybe this belongs to you after all." Madeline thrusts the suitcase at Chase.

"We can keep it?" Ava asks, her face lighting up.

The woman nods.

"Thank you so much!" Chase says. Then he remembers they've spent almost all their money. "But we only have a dollar."

"Just take it." Madeline turns away.

Ava grabs Chase's arm and whispers, "Let's get out of here before she changes her mind."

They walk their bikes to where the flea market blends into the park. The suitcase bangs against Chase's leg. It's heavier than he expected.

"I don't think this is empty," he says as they lean their bikes against a tree and plop down on the grass.

"Time to find out!" Ava replies. She swings open the lid.

They both gasp!

chapter 4

Stranger Things

The suitcase is definitely NOT empty. It is filled with silver-colored foam. Chase presses his finger into it. Squishy, but firm. How strange!

But the foam is not even the strangest part. The strangest part is what is nestled *inside* the foam. There are four rows of objects, each one odder than the next.

Row one holds an uncooked potato, a doorknob in the shape of a dragon's head, a gold cube, and a black stone beetle with a green hexagon-shaped jewel on its back.

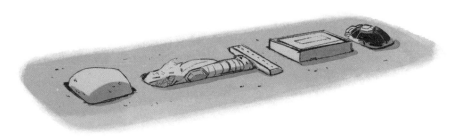

Row two gets even *more* bizarre: a bag of dirt, a white feather, a slim purple candle, and a glass tube.

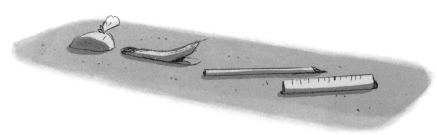

Row three has slots for four more items, but the slots are empty.

Row four holds one item only, and it's the oddest of them all. It looks like a cross between a cell phone and a remote control. But instead of numbers, it has multicolored circular buttons on the front. And there is no ON-OFF switch.

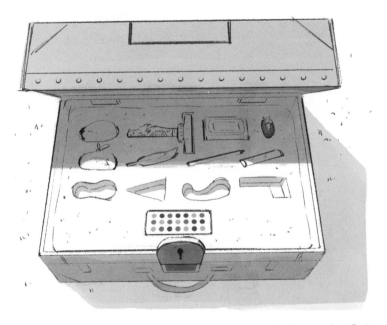

Ava bounces up and down. "Chase! This suitcase is by far the COOLEST thing we've EVER found at the flea market!"

Before Chase can agree, Ava reaches for the beetle. She always did have a thing for bugs.

Chase pushes the suitcase away from her. "Wait!"

She frowns. "Why did you do that?"

"These things look important," Chase says. "We should see if Madeline even knows they're in here. Maybe she'd want them back."

"Fine," Ava grumbles.

As Chase clicks the suitcase closed, they hear angry voices. The shouts are coming from Madeline's booth!

"Where is it?" a tall man in a gray suit shouts at Madeline. "I know you have it! Give me my suitcase!"

The Angry Man

Without realizing it, Chase and Ava move a bit closer to each other. The action at the suitcase booth is heating up!

Madeline's hands are on her hips. She doesn't look happy.

The man keeps shouting, "Where is my suitcase?!"

Madeline finally shouts back, "I don't know what you're talking about! Please leave!"

But he doesn't leave. Instead, he begins opening suitcases and tossing them aside.

"What's he doing?" Ava whispers.

Chase can only guess. "Maybe he is checking to see if his suitcase is hidden inside a bigger one?"

The man shouts again. "You don't know who or what you're dealing with!"

Ava turns to Chase. "Do you think he's looking for *our* suitcase?"

"I hope not," Chase replies. "But should we go check? I mean, if it's really his, shouldn't we give it back?"

"No way!" Ava says. "We bought this suitcase fair and square."

"Actually," Chase points out, "we didn't *buy* it at all."

They watch as the man whips out a cell phone and jabs at it angrily.

Then he stuffs it back in his pocket and stomps around the booth some more.

Chase has seen enough. With one foot, he pushes the suitcase behind the tree. He might not know who the suitcase really belongs to, but he definitely doesn't want *this* guy to have it.

"Thank you," Ava whispers.

"You won't get away with this!" The man yells at Madeline. Then he storms away from the booth.

As soon as he's gone, Madeline turns around. She looks directly at Chase and Ava and mouths the word: **Run!**

chapter 6

Faster!

Chase's heart begins to pound. What should they do? He scans the flea market until he spots the tall man again. Oh no! The man is walking back toward the booth.

Ava is already on her bike. "Come on!" she says. "Let's go!"

Chase springs into action. He grabs the suitcase and hops on his bike. He doesn't want to risk the man seeing them — *or* the suitcase!

They pedal at top speed toward the bike path.

Ava cranes her neck around to see if the man has spotted them, and she almost crashes into Chase!

Steering with one hand while holding the suitcase with the other is not easy. Chase's bike wobbles as they weave their way through the trees and down toward the playground.

After a close call with an evergreen tree, Chase parks his bike next to Ava's. Usually the playground is packed, but he's glad to see it's empty now.

He lays the suitcase down.

They both reach for the lock.

But before either of them can touch it, the suitcase springs open on its own!

"Whoa!" Ava says, wide-eyed.

"I know this sounds crazy," Chase says, "but I think the suitcase is telling us it's ours."

"I think so, too," Ava says.

They stare down at the strange objects.

Ava reaches for the beetle again. When Chase tries to stop her, his arm hits the side of the suitcase. The dragon doorknob pops out of its slot and Chase reaches to catch it.

As soon as he wraps his fingers around it, the ground begins to rumble and shake!

"Is this an earthquake?" Ava calls out, her eyes wild. She quickly shuts the suitcase and grabs the handle.

Ava clings to her brother as the ground begins to spin! Or maybe they're the ones spinning! It's too hard to tell!

Faster and faster they spin! Images blur in front of their eyes — mountains, oceans, cities, and faces!

This is NO earthquake!

chapter 7

Two Bad Knights

When the spinning finally stops, Chase is surprised to see he and Ava are lying on the ground, the suitcase beside them.

But instead of the soft, green grass of the playground, they are sprawled on a cold, hard floor! Wooden boxes line one wall. Mops and brooms lean against another wall.

They are in a closet! The only light comes from a gap beneath the door.

"What just happened, Ava?" Chase asks. "Where *are* we?"

"I have no idea," Ava says, clutching her belly. "But I really wish I hadn't eaten that funnel cake."

Chase holds up the dragon doorknob. "Things started getting all weird and twisty when I touched this." With shaking hands, he opens the suitcase and shoves the doorknob back into its slot.

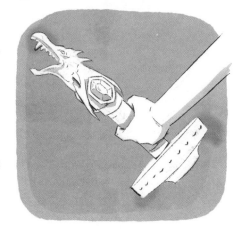

"Maybe this is a dream," Ava suggests. She sticks out her arm. "Pinch me."

Chase squeezes above her elbow.

"Ow!" She rubs her arm. "Okay, we're not dreaming."

"We have to get home," Chase says. They move toward the door, then freeze when they hear the **CLOMP CLOMP** of boots.

Ava reaches out to open the door.

"Stop," Chase hisses.

"Why?" Ava replies. "Maybe whoever is out there can tell us where we are."

Chase points at the large keyhole. They push their heads together and peer through it. They can clearly see two men. The men are dressed in armor and carrying swords on their belts! One has a beard. The other is much younger.

"It is a little early for Halloween," Ava whispers.

Chase shushes her.

"Everything is ready for the tournament today, right?" the younger man asks. "This is one sporting event no one will forget!"

"Indeed," the older man tells the other. "Trust me, no one will ever know we had anything to do with what happens to the young king. He will win his sword fights like always." The man lets out a deep, mean laugh. Then he adds, "Until Big Rob shows up at the tournament!"

"That's right!" the younger man says. "The strange man with two different-colored eyes has made sure that Big Rob's winning streak won't be broken!"

"Haha, *broken*," laughs the bearded man. "Good one."

Chase doesn't move a muscle. Nothing about the knights' conversation sounds funny to him.

The older knight continues, "Being a knight was hard work, but being rich will be easy!"

"And all we had to do to get the money was keep that troublemaking wizard out of the way," the younger knight replies. "Now no one will be able to warn the king!"

The two knights slap each other on the shoulders and **CLOMP CLOMP** out of view.

Chase and Ava move away from the keyhole.

Ava whispers, "Did he just say *wizard*?"

chapter 8

Magic or Not?

"Magic and wizards don't really exist!" Chase says for a third time. They'd been arguing for five minutes already.

"Yes, they do," Ava insists. "Fairies and dragons are real, too. But not monsters or elves."

Chase throws up his hands. "Either way, we need to find out where we are." He peeks through the keyhole. "All clear."

They step out of the closet and almost fall back when they see the room. Giant tapestries hang on the walls, colorful rugs cover the stone floors, and a huge, round table sits in the center of the room.

Ava looks up at a painting of a dragon. A word is spelled out in gold letters above it: **PENDRAGON.**

"See?" she says. "Dragons *are* real. This one has a weird name though."

"That's not the dragon's name," Chase says slowly. He is struggling to make sense of the clues all around him. A wizard and a round table and knights in armor and the name *Pendragon* . . .

Chase has a collection of books at home on medieval Great Britain. He knows exactly who has the last name of Pendragon.

But how is this possible? Magic isn't real! They couldn't have gone back in time!

Or could they have?

Chase takes a deep breath. This *is* real. And for a kid like him who loves history, this is completely amazing.

"Ava," he says in a voice full of wonder. "I know where we are. And I know WHEN we are. We're in *King Arthur's castle* in medieval times! We have gone back over a *thousand years!*"

chapter 9 In Hiding

Chase expects Ava to tell him he's crazy and that there's no way they went back in time. Instead, she looks around, shrugs, and says, "Yeah, that sounds about right. There's one thing I don't get though . . . I thought knights were the good guys?"

"Not all of them, I guess," Chase says. "But I know that King Arthur lived a long life. Those guys said he is still young now. That means we don't have to worry — the knights' plan doesn't work!"

"But what if you're wrong?" Ava asks. "Shouldn't we warn the king? It sounds like he could get really hurt."

Chase shakes his head. "Trust me. Time travel doesn't work that way. If we butt in, we could mess up the timeline. History could unravel like a ball of yarn. We can't get involved."

"Since when do you know so much about time travel?" Ava demands.

He crosses his arms. "I've read a few books."

"But what if the whole reason we're here is to save the king?" Ava argues.

"We are not here for any reason," Chase replies. "We're here by accident. Because of the suitcase."

The suitcase! Chase darts back into the closet and tucks it behind a crate labeled PICKLED PLUMS.

"The suitcase will be safer here than out in plain sight with us," he tells Ava.

"Where are we going?" she asks.

"To watch the tournament with everyone else," Chase replies. "We'll get to see King Arthur *in real life*!"

"Okay," Ava says, "but we'll stand out dressed like this."

"You're right," Chase says. "We need to borrow some clothes."

Looking both ways first, they race up a large stone staircase.

Fortunately, the first bedroom they peek into is empty and the closet door is wide open. Along with a lot of dresses, there is one white shirt with long, puffy sleeves. They both reach for that one, but Chase grabs it first.

Ava grumbles about having to wear a dress, but she is soon twirling around the room in one she slipped over her clothes. It's long enough to hide the tips of her colorful sneakers.

Chase has just pulled on his poufy shirt when — **CREAK!**

The bedroom door begins to open!

"Let's clean this room first," a woman's voice says from the hall. A second woman agrees.

Chase pulls Ava down and they crawl under the bed.

"Why are we hiding?" Ava whispers. "We have the right clothes now."

"Because we still can't risk messing up the timeline," Chase says, pinching his nose to keep from sneezing. It's so dusty! At least they know no one cleans under here!

Four feet in brown lace-up shoes walk over to the bed. Chase and Ava scoot closer to the center, praying neither woman looks underneath.

"I cannot wait for the tournament today!" one of them says as she fluffs the blanket. "Four men signed up to challenge the king. They will not win, of course."

"No one can beat Excalibur," the other maid agrees.

Chase's ears perk up at the mention of Excalibur. He loves the story of how King Arthur got his sword. Excalibur's blade was stuck in a rock, and no one could pull it out until Arthur came along. It slid right out in his hand like it had been waiting for him.

That's how finding the suitcase had felt to Chase and Ava!

"King Arthur beats his opponents because of his strength and skill," the first maid argues. "Excalibur doesn't have anything to do with it."

"Perhaps you're right," the other says as they tidy the closet. "Now let's hurry. The tournament starts in less than one hour."

Chase waits until the door closes behind the women. Then he nudges Ava and they slide out from under the bed.

"Look!" Ava cries.

He follows her gaze to a giant portrait on the wall. It had been hidden by the closet door.

"That's the king," Chase says. "And he is holding the famous sword the maids were talking about."

"I know," Ava says impatiently, "but look closer! Look at the handle!"

"It's called a hilt," Chase tells her. Then he gasps.

ARTHUR PENDRAGON

The sword's hilt is carved into the shape of a dragon. It looks just like the dragon doorknob from their suitcase!

chapter 11

A Secret Door

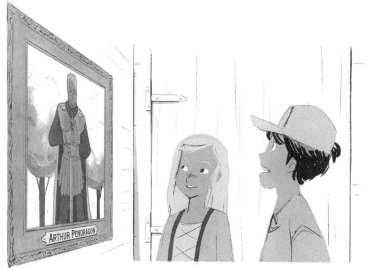

ARTHUR PENDRAGON

The dragon doorknob is NOT a doorknob after all!

"How did Excalibur's hilt get into our suitcase?" Chase asks. "King Arthur's sword is supposed to be unbreakable. Who broke it?"

"*Broken!*" Ava repeats. "That's why those knights laughed at that word. *They* must've broken it!"

Chase shakes his head. "Remember how they were talking about a man with two different-colored eyes? It sounded like *he* did it."

"Let's go find him!" Ava insists. "If *he* broke Excalibur and sent the hilt into the future, then he must know how to get us home!"

"There's no time," Chase says. "If King Arthur doesn't have Excalibur all in one piece, he might lose the sword fight with Big Rob! And if he gets seriously hurt — or worse — that would change the whole course of history! Maybe it really IS up to us to fix this." An uneasy thought enters Chase's mind. "Unless . . . Oh no!"

"What is it?" Ava asks.

"What if the man at the flea market was trying to get the hilt back to Arthur *before* the tournament? Maybe *that's* why he was so worked up when he couldn't find the suitcase. He could be a good guy . . . We might have ruined everything by taking it."

Ava grabs his arm. "Maybe you're right. But we're here now, and we have the hilt. So let's go get the suitcase and fix this!"

As soon as they open the bedroom door, voices and laughter from downstairs make them shut it again. They can't risk going out the way they came in.

"In my books there are always secret passageways inside old castles," Chase says. "We could use one of those right now."

Ava feels along the wall.

Her hand slides under the king's portrait. "I found something!"

The painting itself is a door! She swings it open to reveal a winding stone staircase.

"Beginner's luck," Chase says with a grin.

The staircase only goes up! Chase hopes it will meet up with another staircase that goes down. He takes a deep breath and leads the way.

They're both breathing hard when they reach a dead end. Light peeks through the edges of the stones. They wedge their hands into the tiny gaps. The stones shift slightly.

"Push!" Ava says. "There is definitely something on the other side!"

They try again and again, pressing
on different stones,
and —

CRASH! The stones fall forward, and
Chase and Ava tumble after them.

They scramble to their feet. They're in a small, round room with a glass ceiling. There is a white-haired man in a pointed purple hat standing behind a desk piled high with books.

"Come for another card trick?" the man grumbles.

The White-Haired Wizard

chapter 12

"**We** love card tricks!" Ava says.

The white-haired man whirls around. His face is creased with deep lines, but his eyes are bright and clear.

"You're Merlin!" Chase exclaims. "You're King Arthur's famous wizard!"

The old man tips his pointy hat at them. "The one and only. And I see now you're not those two greedy knights who locked me in my own library."

Merlin glances over at the big hole in the wall. "Thank you for providing my escape route!" he says. "So, who are you and why are you here?"

Chase is too starstruck to answer.

Ava steps forward. "I'm Ava, and this is my brother, Chase. We're from the future and we've come to save King Arthur."

Chase quickly finds his voice. "What she means is, well, I guess that's pretty much right."

They spill out their story, starting from finding the suitcase. At the end, Ava shows Merlin her tie-dyed sneakers as proof they're from the future.

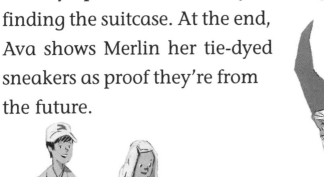

"I have never heard a tale such as that," Merlin says. "But I believe you. I knew that the man with one brown eye and one green must have powerful magic to have broken the king's sword."

"Isn't your magic stronger than anyone else's?" Chase asks.

Merlin shakes his head. "I can't compete with powers I don't understand. Besides, I couldn't even break free from this room." Then he brightens. "But no matter! I am free now. I must go warn the king of the plot against him."

"We want to help," Chase says.

"You two get the hilt and meet me on the castle lawn," Merlin says. "I will try to use my magic to repair Excalibur. We must hurry!" With a swirl of his robe, he rushes into the staircase.

Ava follows, with Chase right behind.

Soon, they burst back into the bedroom. Everyone must be outside for the tournament, because it is quiet in the castle now.

Chase and Ava hurry downstairs to the closet.

Chase grabs the suitcase from its hiding place. He quickly opens it and removes the hilt. He shoves it into his pocket.

Then they're out the castle door. Ava does her best to hide the suitcase in the folds of her dress.

"Look for Merlin and try to blend in," Chase whispers as he and his sister join the crowd streaming onto the lawn.

"The king will be arriving soon!" he hears one woman tell another.

Ava lowers her head and whispers to Chase, "I hope we don't bump into the people whose clothes we borrowed!"

Just then, she bumps into a tall man and knocks his hat sideways!

"Hey, watch where you're going!" the man scolds. He pulls his hat low and scowls at them before pushing deeper into the crowd.

Chase and Ava stop in their tracks. Chase tries to make sense of what he just saw.

The angry man in the hat is the same angry guy from the flea market!

And he has two different-colored eyes!

chapter 13

Let the Games Begin!

"So let me get this straight," Ava says, stepping away from the crowd. "The man who wanted our suitcase in the future is *the same man* who broke King Arthur's sword in the past?"

"Yes!" Chase says. "And that means he most definitely *isn't* a good guy. We need to tell Merlin he's here!"

Before they can move —

BRUMP BRUMP BRAH! A loud trumpet blows.

A hush falls over the crowd as a white horse trots onto the field. A kind-faced young man in a gold crown waves from the horse's back. "Long live King Arthur!" the crowd shouts.

Chase can't help it. He gasps. Never in his wildest dreams could he have imagined standing under the same sky as the real King Arthur!

As the king climbs down from the horse, the two knights they'd overheard earlier place a large golden box next to him. Chase spots the man with the two different-colored eyes watching from beside a tree.

"Excalibur! Excalibur!" the crowd cheers.

Arthur opens the box. He lifts out the sword — but it's only the blade!

Arthur's jaw drops. Then he gently places the blade back in the box.

King Arthur strides to the center of the field. He holds a shield in one hand and pulls a regular-looking sword from the side of his belt. His eyes narrow. "I will find out who broke Excalibur. But first, I will battle my opponents as planned. Let the tournament begin!"

Three men line up across from the king. Then a fourth man steps forward. He towers over everyone else. His shoulders are as wide as two regular-sized men!

"That must be Big Rob," Ava whispers.

Chase nods.

King Arthur begins to battle the first opponent. He swings and thrusts with his sword. The blades and shields clang and clash until the king knocks the sword out of the man's hand.

The man bows and the crowd cheers. This happens again with the second opponent, and with the third.

Chase and Ava look at each other. Maybe the king will win after all.

Finally, Big Rob steps up to take his turn. The crowd goes quiet. The sword fight starts out like the others. In less than a minute though, the king's sword is flung from his hand. And Big Rob keeps swinging!

Arthur raises his shield to protect himself.

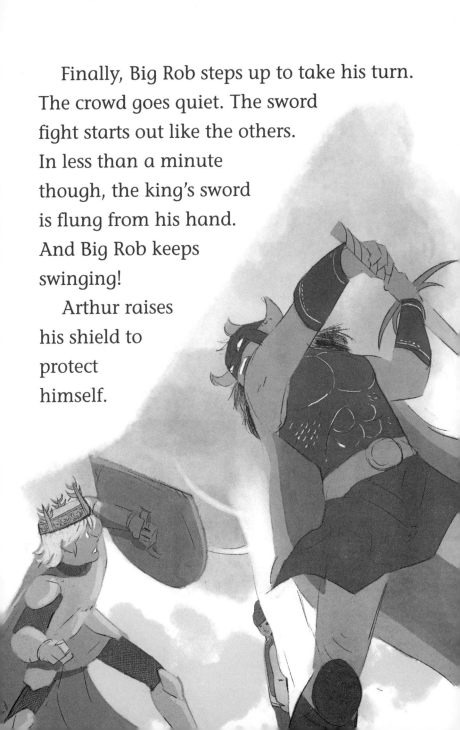

Chase starts to panic. He scans the crowd. The two knights have disappeared. The man from the flea market is still by the tree, smiling as he watches the battle.

Where is Merlin?

CLASH! Big Rob takes a chunk out of the king's shield.

Chase turns to his sister and holds up the hilt. "It's time to mess with the timeline!"

chapter 14

The Battle

Chase darts through the crowd, keeping one eye on the action and the other on the box with Excalibur's blade in it.

King Arthur rolls out of the way just as Big Rob's sword strikes the ground inches from Arthur's head!

The man with the different-colored eyes is next to the box now. But he is looking the other way. Chase should still be able to grab the blade. Holding his breath, Chase brushes his fingers against the cold steel.

But before he can get a solid grip on it, the man steps between him and the box.

"What do you think you're doing?" he asks. Then he spots the hilt in Chase's hand and his eyes go wide.

"It was you!" the man shouts. "*You* stole my suitcase!"

Chase turns to run, but the man grabs him by the collar.

Chase has to think fast! He raises his arms over his head. The poufy shirt he's wearing slides right off!

Chase grabs the blade before the man can react. He starts running. The blade is so heavy he needs both hands to carry it.

Chase risks a glance over his shoulder. The man is only a few steps behind.

Ava appears at Chase's side. The suitcase bangs against her legs and she stumbles. Chase catches her just as a hand grazes his neck. But before the man can get a firm grip, Merlin is between them!

"Sorry I'm late!" the wizard says, throwing his hands up to the sky.

A loud thunderclap fills the air, followed by a plume of smoke. It looks like Merlin *does* know a real magic trick or two!

People begin running in all directions. In the chaos, the man from the flea market is swallowed up by the crowd and the smoke.

But the battle between King Arthur and Big Rob rages on! Big Rob brings down his sword. The king's shield goes flying!

Chase quickly thrusts the hilt and blade at Merlin. "Attach them — *please!*"

A yellow glow rises up from the wizard's hands. But nothing else happens. He shakes his head. "My magic is not strong enough."

Chase is stunned. On the field, Big Rob raises his sword and is about to strike. Chase tugs on Merlin's long robe. "But King Arthur needs Excalibur right now!"

Merlin hands the blade to Chase and the hilt to Ava. "I cannot do it," he tells them. "But *you* can."

Chase and Ava begin to argue with the wizard. Then Chase thinks of how well he and Ava worked together at the flea market that morning. As though reading his mind, Ava says, "We're a team."

Chase brings the end of the blade down onto the hilt.

Time seems to slow. They hold their breath as the hilt and the blade knit together, strands of steel twisting and blending into one. For an instant the whole sword glows red, then hardens. Excalibur is whole again.

"How did we *do* that?" Ava asks in a whisper.

"I have no idea," Chase says. "We can figure that out later. But now —" He whirls around and shouts, "CATCH!"

Then he lobs the sword right at King Arthur.

chapter 15

Saving a King

King Arthur catches Excalibur just in time. He thrusts the sword upward to block Big Rob's blow. Then he keeps on swinging. Within seconds, the huge man's sword is torn from his grip.

The king holds up Excalibur in one hand and grabs on to Big Rob's wrist with the other.

King Arthur has won!
The crowd cheers! Chase
and Ava shout along with
everyone else. They did it!

Ava pulls her camera out from under her collar. *Click.* She tucks it away again before anyone can see. Then she says, "I had hoped that once the sword was fixed we'd be sent home."

"Me, too," Chase admits. He pauses. "Do you hear a humming sound?"

"Yes! I thought I heard something," Ava says. "But with all the cheering going on I couldn't tell for sure. I think it's coming from in there!" Ava points to the suitcase.

They hurry away from the crowd, then open it. The humming gets louder.

The remote control is buzzing and the red button is lit up!

Ava reaches for the remote, but —

"Wait!" a voice shouts. Chase and Ava look up. The man from the flea market is coming right toward them! But he is not alone.  King Arthur and Merlin lead the way, while two of the king's guards hold the man's arms.

"Give me my suitcase!" the man shouts at Chase and Ava as the group arrives.

"You are not in a position to make demands!" the king booms. "For the last time, tell me your name!"

The man shakes his head. The king steps closer.

Then the man mumbles, "Randall."

"Well, Randall, I hope you enjoy your stay in our dungeon," the king says.

"Don't worry," Merlin adds. "You'll have two greedy knights and Big Rob to keep you company."

"Not for long," Randall says under his breath.

The king puts his hands on Chase's and Ava's shoulders. "Thank you both for your bravery today. Merlin and I shall never forget it. What can I give you for your kindness?"

"We can't take anything where we're going," Chase says.

"Sure we can!" Ava replies.

"No, we can't," Chase insists. Then he whispers to his sister, "Look what happened the last time someone took something out of the timeline."

The humming remote begins to jump toward Ava's hand. She lifts it up. The red button is now pulsing. She and Chase grab for each other. Then she presses the button.

The ground instantly begins to spin!

"Goodbye, Merlin! Goodbye, King Arthur!" they shout.

"Thanks for the dress!" Ava adds, pulling it off and tossing it behind her.

Medieval Great Britain disappears into a swirl of sky and earth. The last thing they hear is a furious voice shouting, "I'll find you, Time Jumpers! That suitcase is mine!"

chapter 16

Home Sweet Home

When the spinning stops, Chase sees people walking toward the playground with bags from the flea market. And the sun is still bright in the sky! Even though they were at the castle all day, it's still late afternoon here. They haven't even missed dinner!

"That really happened..." Ava whispers. "We went back in time!" The remote in her hand has gone silent and dark once again. She locks it in the suitcase.

"And now we're back!" Chase shouts. He wants to dance and sing. Instead, he leans over and hugs his sister —  something he hasn't done since she lost her part in the second-grade play. "If I had to get stuck back in time with anyone, I'm glad it was you."

Ava blushes. "Yeah, me, too." She looks over at the suitcase. "What do you think that guy Randall meant when he called us Time Jumpers?"

"No idea," Chase says. "We'll have to find Madeline at the flea market next weekend. We need to know how Randall found us. I have a feeling she knows more than she let on."

As they bike home, Chase says, "Maybe we shouldn't tell anyone about all this until we understand more about it. Even Mom and Dad. We don't want to worry them."

Ava hesitates, then says, "Agreed."

They hear their parents in the kitchen. "We're home!" they shout, then run upstairs.

Chase slides the suitcase under his bed. Then he pulls out his favorite notebook. He needs to write down every detail about medieval Great Britain.

A few minutes later, Ava comes in and hands him the picture frame she bought at the flea market. "To remember our adventure." She'd printed out the photo of King Arthur and slid it into the frame.

"Thanks!" he says, admiring the picture of the real live King Arthur. Amazing! Chase places it on his night table so it will be the first thing he sees every morning.

"I was thinking about something," he tells Ava. "I don't think that was a cell phone that Randall was using at the flea market earlier. I think he has a remote control like ours."

Ava's eyes widen. "You must be right! Our remote knew it was time to send us home as soon as the dragon hilt was back where it belonged. Randall must have been checking his matching remote at the flea market to see if anything inside the suitcase had been returned!"

"Exactly," Chase says. "Let's make sure we never leave our remote behind."

Ava looks at her brother in surprise. "You mean we're going back in time again?"

"I don't think we have a choice," he says. "There are a lot more things in that suitcase. Maybe they all need to go somewhere. We're Time Jumpers, right?"

Ava grins. "Right!"

From under the bed, the suitcase begins to rattle.

WENDY MASS

has written several award-winning series for young readers including the **Willow Falls** series, *Twice Upon a Time, Space Taxi,* and *The Candymakers*. She recently learned that you can travel back in time every night just by looking up at the sky! The light from stars takes so long to reach us that any star you see is in the past. How cool is that? Wendy and her family live in a rural part of New Jersey. They have two cats and a dog, all of whom she calls her son's name by mistake.

ORIOL VIDAL

is an illustrator and storyboard artist who lives in Barcelona, Spain, with his wife, daughter, and a cat named Lana. He always wanted to be a "painter" when he grew up. Finally, his hobby became his job! Time Jumpers is the first early chapter book series he has illustrated. When Oriol is not drawing, he likes to travel with his family all over the world. And in his dreams, he time travels to the past . . . just like the Time Jumpers!

Time Jumpers

Questions and Activities

STEALING THE SWORD

1. Who gives Chase and Ava the suitcase? What does this woman have in common with Chase?

2. Chase knows a lot about time travel. What does he mean when he says, "We could mess up the timeline"? Turn back to page 41.

3. Chase and Ava spot Randall at the flea market *and* at the castle. How does Randall travel through time? Why do *you* think he wants the suitcase?

4. King Arthur's famous sword is called Excalibur. Chase recalls the story of the sword on page 47. Using books and the Internet, research more about the legend of King Arthur. Write and draw pictures to share what you learn.

5. Chase and Ava travel back in time to medieval Great Britain. What are some ways life in the medieval times was different from life today? Would you want to live back then? Why or why not?